First impression: May 1989
© Y Lolfa 1989

Illustrations: Helen Holmes

ISBN: 0 86243 182 4

Printed and published in Wales
by Y Lolfa Cyf., Talybont, Dyfed SY24 5HE;
Talybont (097086) 304

# Contents

CLWYD

Llangollen

POWYS

GWENT

Caerdydd

MORGANNWG

Llyn Syfaddan
Llangasty
Llyn-y-Fan Fach
Myddfai

GWYNEDD

Eryri
Yr Wyddfa
Nant Gwynant
Beddgelert
Harlech
Nannau
Aberystwyth

Afon Erch

Tai
Eddin
Llannerch-y-medd
Aberffrawl
Abermenai

Llŷn

DYFED

Llanarthne

Glyn Rhosyn

# How Snowdon was Built in a Day

*In* those long ago days when King Arthur was still a child, there lived in Britain two very vain kings. They spent their time lording it over their subjects. When they had a minute or two to spare, they vied with each other for supremacy. One king strutted before the other king, all puffed up with pride and fit to burst, boasting of his wealth and titles. The two kings were so conceited, they didn't care what they said so long as it sounded better than what they heard.

One morning, they were riding across the fields together. The king who owned the land puffed out his chest and said: 'I bet you've never, ever in your whole life, ridden across such large fields as these. They're bigger and better than any you've seen anywhere in the whole wide world, and that's a fact!'

The other king felt his head swell and he said: 'I can see that you are a hopeless judge of fields. My own land is fifty times better than this little paddock of yours. You must come and see it sometime—it will be a real eye-opener for you.'

The first king was peeved. 'Just look at my flocks,' he said pointing to the four corners of the earth. 'Did you ever see so many perfect horses and flocks in all your born days?'

'Oh, yes,' said his rival. 'I look out at them from my castle rooms every morning and again at night. They're all mine, every horse's mane and sheep's fleece that I see.'

'Well, I never saw such a con-

7

ceited, stuck-up king,' said the first king. 'But you meet me here on this very field of mine tonight after dark, and I'll show you the finest field ever. No king living or dead or of the fairies ever had such a field as the one I'll show you tonight.' At that, the two stiff-necked kings parted.

They met again on that same night, at exactly the same spot, in exactly the same mood.

'Just look at my best field,' said the first king. 'You'll never own such a wonderful expanse of field as that one.'

'I can't see it,' said the second king. 'It must be too small for me to see.'

'Look up at the sky,' said the first king. 'There's my field in all its grandeur. It is everywhere—as far as you can see in every direction, and it's all mine.'

'Oh, yes, of course,' said the second king. 'That field there where my herds and flocks graze. Thank you for the grazing rights. My animals have grown fat on your land.'

'Animals? Your animals in my field? Where? Show me at once!' demanded the angry king.

'There they are, all over the field, in every nook and corner. They cover the whole wide sky. Some call them stars, galaxies—call them what you will—but they're my sheep and cattle glowing in the light of the moon, and that's mine too!'

The first king stared at the star-spangled sky and at the quiet moon guarding it.

'You sly, wicked king,' said the

first king. 'Hustle your animals out of my field this instant.'

'Indeed I won't,' said the second king.

'Yes you will,' bellowed one.

'No I won't,' sniggered the other.

'Yes!' thundered the one.

'No!' roared the other.

One thing led to another and, in no time at all, they were brawling like little brats and, before anyone knew anything, their two kingdoms were at war.

Rhita the Giant soon came to know of their quarrel. Rhita the Giant was King of North Wales. He was eager to stop the war being waged by the two vain kings.

'And in any case,' said Rhita, 'I own the skies and all its flocks and herds.'

Now Rhita was not vain, but he was certainly mean. He skimped and scraped and would even stop one hole in a sieve if he thought he could make a saving. Not for Rhita such stories of vain kings, hoarding treasures in the sky.

Rhita gathered together his armies and soon had the two lesser kings under his thumb. As punishment, he had the two kings' beards shorn off in one piece, stitched the beards together, and wore them on his head to keep his skull warm as he walked his land at night, looking at his vast new field, and all its herds and flocks.

But that is far from being the end of the story. There were more than three kings in Britain. And the other kings were not happy that Rhita the Giant was throwing his weight about in such a shameful way—disbearding kings being a very serious action indeed. Who would be the next to lose his beard? It was a great insult. These angry kings assembled their armies and marched against Rhita the Giant. But Rhita was ready and waiting for them. He put an end to their uprising in a mere five minutes. It took Rhita's barber far longer to shave off so many kings' beards in one piece, and it took Rhita's tailor that much longer again to sew them together, to make a mantle for Rhita to walk the fields at night, looking at his not-so-new field and count its herds and flocks.

By now Rhita was an avid beard-collector. If he heard of a new king who wore a beard, Rhita couldn't rest until he had that beard, too, in his mantle. Of course, the time soon came when his mantle could grow no more without tripping up its owner, so the collecting had to come to a stop. Rhita needed only one more beard to complete his mantle, and that space was at the very bottom of the hemline. Who's beard would fit that space? Alas, there were no bearded kings left in Britain.

Soon, Rhita heard of the death of one of the kings of the south. A new, young king took his place. The new king was King Arthur.

'I must have King Arthur's beard to complete my mantle,' said Rhita. 'It will fit perfectly.'

Rhita sent a message down to the new king telling him to shave off his beard and send it up to Rhita the Giant, King of North Wales, who needed it to patch his cloak.

King Arthur was quite disgusted.

'What nonsense is this?' he asked his soldiers. King Arthur's men told him of Rhita's cloak of beards.

'I know of just the right beard to patch his cloak with,' said the young king, 'but if Rhita wants mine, then he'd better come and fight me for it.'

Rhita's messenger returned to his master with King Arthur's reply. Rhita was very angry. 'How dare he disobey me!' he raged. Now Rhita would have to spend his money on sending his armies all the way south to fetch Arthur's beard. But pay he would!

As Rhita and his armies approached King Arthur's lands, they saw flashing lights all along the boundary of King Arthur's realm. As they got nearer, they heard a crashing roar that filled the skies with a tremor.

'What's that light and this terrible noise?' asked the Giant.

'Oh, the light is only the armour of King Arthur's knights flashing in the sun. The roaring and the tremor is the sound of the knights greeting King Arthur as he approaches them,' said the Giant's spies.

'Oh! Is that so!' Rhita said with a tremble.

Soon a sweet smell wafted on the air towards Rhita and his soldiers.

'What's that sweet smell that fills the air?' asked Rhita.

'Oh, that's only King Arthur and his men drinking mead,' said one of Rhita's spies. 'They always drink mead before a battle. It makes them stronger. If one of King Arthur's men strikes you after he has drunk that mead, it's as if nine men have given you a blow.'

'Oh! Is that so!' said trembling Rhita.

It was soon time to proceed to the battlefield. King Arthur and Rhita the Giant met with their two armies on a level plain. Rhita was still shaking like a leaf.

'I think we'll yield,' said Rhita limply.

'What a disappointment,' smiled King Arthur. 'But I won't disappoint you as to that beard. You'll get your patch of beard all right!'

'You'll give me your beard?' asked the wide-eyed Rhita.

'No, I'll give you yours,' said King Arthur.

One of King Arthur's men had a flaying-knife handy and he flayed off Rhita's beard, there and then. The beard was stitched in place right at the very edge of the hem of Rhita's cloak. To his shame, Rhita had to wear his cloak of beards for the rest of his days.

Had Rhita obeyed King Arthur and lived a peaceful life in North Wales, maybe he would still be there today. As it was, King Arthur and Rhita the Giant had another difference of opinion. King Arthur marched his men against the Giant. With one flash of Arthur's sword, Rhita the Giant was slain. King Arthur then commanded his soldiers each to put one stone on the dead Giant's body—and that is how Snowdon was built in a day.

# Prince Culhwch

A long time ago, there lived a prince with a strange name. The prince's name was Culhwch. There was another strange thing about him. He could only marry one of two women. His wife would have to be either his stepmother's daughter, or Olwen, a cruel giant's daughter. Of the two, he preferred Olwen, although he had never seen her and didn't even know where she lived. No-one seemed to know.

At last Culhwch's father had a brainwave. 'Ask your cousin, King Arthur, about her. He should know.'

'Good idea,' said Culhwch. He set off to Arthur's court riding a smart, grey stallion. He carried with him two silver spears, a battle-axe that would draw blood from the wind, a golden sword, and a shield the colour of lightning. Culhwch wore a plush purple mantle with four gold brooches on it, each one worth a hundred cows. Culhwch's greyhounds went with him to Arthur's court. They had white breasts, and wore collars of thick gold.

When they arrived at the gates of King Arthur's court, the porter was very impressed. But he was such a surly porter, he almost refused to let Culhwch in through the gates. Culhwch was so desperate to know where Olwen lived, he threatened the porter.

'If you don't let me in, I'll scream so loudly, they'll hear me from Cornwall to Ireland,' said Culhwch.

'You make as much noise as you like, son. I'll still have to consult

King Arthur,' was all the rude porter would say. He went inside.

On his return, he was slightly more civil-tongued. Culhwch was allowed in. But King Arthur had never heard of Olwen! Culhwch was very disappointed. However, King Arthur volunteered to send messengers to look for Olwen while Culhwch stayed at Arthur's court. Soldiers spent the whole year searching for Olwen, but were none the wiser for all their efforts.

Culhwch almost sulked, and would have done so if Cai hadn't taken things in hand. Cai had special powers. Under water, he could hold his breath for nine days and nights; no doctor could heal a blow from Cai's sword; if Cai wished, he could grow as tall as the highest tree; however much it rained, Cai had so much heat in his body that whatever he held in his hand remained as dry as a cork. When his friends were cold, Cai's heat could kindle a fire for them to toast their toes by, and warm their noses. Culhwch was proud to have such a skilful friend.

'You're wrong to blame Arthur for not finding Olwen,' Cai said. 'Why don't you come with us to look for her?'

And so began the great search. Eventually they came across a shepherd who knew all about Olwen. The shepherd's wife washed Olwen's hair for her every Saturday, regular as clockwork. Olwen was very beautiful. She wore a dress of red silk, and wore a golden necklace with pearls and rubies in it. Everyone who saw her fell in love with her. Wherever she walked, four white clover flowers grew in her footprint. Culhwch loved hearing tales about Olwen.

'My advice to you is this,' said the shepherd's wife. 'Whatever Olwen's father tells you to do, promise him that you will do it.' Culhwch would do anything to marry Olwen.

When Culhwch and his friends arrived at the giant's castle, Ysbaddaden Chief Giant was in a bad mood.

'Where are my hopeless servants?' he roared. 'Someone push the forks under my eyelids to hitch them up. I want to see my future son-in-law.' Ysbaddaden didn't like the sight.

Three times Culhwch and his friends had to go to the castle before Ysbaddaden would even tell them what they had to do in order to win Olwen for Culhwch. But when he did announce the tasks, they were very difficult. Ysbaddaden wanted to hear Teirtu's harp play at the wedding feast. Teirtu's harp played all by itself without anyone near it, and stopped playing when everyone had had enough of its music. Ysbaddaden also wanted Culhwch to bring Rhiannon's magic birds to sing to him on that night. Rhiannon's birds awoke the dead, and cast a sleeping spell over the living. Ysbaddaden had arranged dozens of difficult tasks for Culhwch and his friends.

'And another thing,' said Ysbaddaden. 'When I shave, ready for the wedding, my beard must be softened only with the Black Witch's blood. You'll never get it.'

'You think these tasks are difficult,' said Culhwch, 'but for me and my friends, they're as simple as can be.

Culhwch wasn't quite sure whether he was telling the truth, but away he went, with his list of tasks in his pocket.

Everything went well. That is to say, everything went well until Culhwch came to the last task—collecting the blood of the Black Witch. He had many adventures and many a fright before ever seeing the Witch, but she was his biggest problem, although Twrch Trwyth was bad enough. Many of King Arthur's soldiers who had come to help Culhwch hunt Twrch Trwyth had perished on his tusks. Twrch Trwyth was a wild boar who carried a comb and scissors between his ears—the very comb and scissors that Ysbaddaden wanted to use to style

his hair for the wedding. Twrch Trwyth wouldn't give them to Culhwch, so Culhwch had to steal them from him.

The Black Witch wouldn't give him her blood either, and no wonder! Culhwch would have to steal that too. King Arthur knew very well where she lived. It was a black, smoky cave in the depths of nowhere. As they neared the cave, King Arthur decided that the two brothers, Cacamwri and Hygwydd, should fight the Witch and take her blood. They both crept stealthily into the blackness, but the Witch's yellow eyes had noticed them. She grabbed hold of Hygwydd by the hair on his head and beat him into the floor under her feet. Cacamwri grabbed hold of the Witch by *her* hair. Cacamwri dragged her from

Hygwydd, and pulled her to the floor. The Witch then turned on Cacamwri. She gave both brothers a good hiding and sent them helter-skelter out of her cave.

King Arthur was beside himself. He wanted to kill the Witch, right there and then. However, he was persuaded to let two other men do the job. Well, if the first two couldn't do it, neither could these. Out they came in blood and tears. All four had to be bundled on the back of King Arthur's horse, and sent home.

King Arthur himself then seized the entrance to the cave. From the door, he aimed at the Witch with Carnwennan, his knife, and slew the Witch through her stomach until she was in two pieces. There was blood everywhere. Caw took back with

him a gallon to soften Ysbaddaden's beard.

Back at Ysbaddaden's castle, he shaved Ysbaddaden's beard, his skin and his flesh clean to the bone, as well as shaving off his two ears.

'You've shaved me well enough now,' said Ysbaddaden. 'Culhwch may marry Olwen.'

But the story doesn't end there. The very minute that the Chief Giant's daughter married, her father had to die. So Ysbaddaden was dragged outside and his head was cut off. And that is the end of the story.

# The Giant of Gilfach

No-one has seen a real giant in Wales for quite some time now but, in the olden days, they were to be seen two-a-penny in the Welsh mountains. They lived in large caves. It was when they wanted to sleep that the trouble began, for then, their feet stuck out a good yard into the snow. The colder their feet became, the meaner the giants grew. So, as a rule, the taller the giant, the more cruel he turned out to be.

The tallest of all the giants was the Giant of Gilfach. He was a mountain of a man, long-limbed and massive. His feet were icy cold. His big toes were frostbitten, and he had six chilblains on each heel. No wonder everyone was afraid of him. He was the cruellest giant that ever lived. His main hobby was stealing children from their warm beds, and eating them alive.

During the winter, he rambled about the mountain forests like a madman, especially when the icy wind drove the snow along the mountain ranges. Then, the Giant of Gilfach uprooted trees by the dozen and carried them to his cave to throw on the fire. But nothing he could do made the slightest difference to his feet, and he was still the same fierce, savage giant that he had always been.

Near the forest where the Giant of Gilfach collected his firewood, there lived a little boy named Hywel. The little boy was an orphan. The Giant had killed Hywel's father and, soon after, Hywel's mother disappeared. Hywel felt sure that it was the Giant of Gilfach that had caught her and fried her in butter for his supper.

Hywel was determined that someone should put a stop to the Giant's rampages. But who? Everyone was afraid of going near the Giant's cave. There was nothing for it but for Hywel to kill the Giant of Gilfach single handed.

For weeks on end, all Hywel did was search the mountains for the Giant of Gilfach, but the Giant kept himself to himself all through that winter. When spring came, Hywel heard one day that someone had seen the Giant. He had only seen him from afar, but he knew that it was the Giant of Gilfach because he had no clothes on. There wasn't a bit of clothing in the land that would

fit the Giant of Gilfach, so he grew his hair long and that kept him from freezing.

This piece of news about the Giant drove Hywel to look again for his enemy. He had no luck. He couldn't find the Giant of Gilfach anywhere. He was so sad and disappointed that he sat on a rock and cried his heart out. Soon, a little man came up to Hywel. The man had heard Hywel crying and wondered what was troubling him.

'I'm looking for the cruel Giant who killed my mother and father,' said Hywel.

'How do you know that it was the Giant who killed them?' asked the kind little man. 'They may have had a bad accident, or maybe they just lost their way on the mountain,' he said.

'Oh, no. My mother saw the Giant of Gilfach kill my father. Now my mother has disappeared too, and what else could have happened to her but that the Giant has taken her also? He steals children too. But I'm going to kill the Giant of Gilfach before he kills me.'

'How will you do that? He's as big as a mountain.'

'I don't know how indeed. I haven't even seen him yet.' Hywel was very sad.

'Have you seen the owl that sits in the crook of that tree?' asked the kind man.

'Yes, it's been there ever since my mother disappeared,' said Hywel. 'I listen to it hooting every night.'

'That owl is the only one who can kill the Giant of Gilfach,' said the man.

'How do you know that?' asked Hywel.

'I can speak to the birds,' said the kind little man.

Hywel was sure that the man must be one of the fairies. Hywel cheered up no end.

'I'll help the owl to do it,' said Hywel and slapped his knee like a very determined cowboy. 'Tell me what to do,' said Hywel.

'All you have to do,' said the man, 'is to leave a strongbow and two arrows in the branches of the tree where the owl hoots at night. Once you've done that, go back to bed, and in the morning come back to the tree. There will be a surprise waiting for you there.'

Hywel returned home. He went up into the attic and found his father's strongbow. When it was getting dark, he crept in the half-light to the owl's tree. He climbed it, and put the strongbow and the two arrows on the top branches. He hoped the old man wasn't joking. Very quickly, Hywel sped back home and went to bed.

But the old man knew exactly what he was doing. He *was* one of the fairies and the Giant of Gilfach had snatched six of the fairies and had killed all six of them. The little man had been watching the Giant for a long time, and knew that he often rested under the owl's tree when he stalked about at night, stealing fleshy children.

On this night, the Giant of Gilfach was up to no good. He had stolen two children and came to rest under the tree where the owl was hooting. Soon, the Giant was fast asleep. As soon as the owl could hear the Giant's deep snores, the owl flew to the top of the tree, picked up the strongbow and one arrow, and aimed carefully at the Giant's heart. She pulled hard, and the next minute the arrow shot through the branches and through the Giant's heart, killing him instantly.

The owl flew down to see the Giant's body, and the kind little man also ran up to see it. The man had a wand in his hand, and he struck the owl with it. The owl turned into a beautiful woman, no other than Hywel's mother.

By now, dawn was breaking and Hywel was waking up. He ran to the tree, and was surprised indeed to see his mother alive and well, and the Giant of Gilfach cold and dead.

# The Hairy Man's Cave

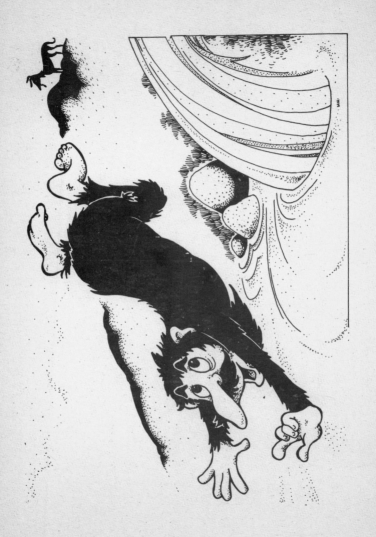

*If* ever you walk the Eryri mountains in Gwynedd, you might just see the river Erch. It sweeps along its river bed, and then tips itself over a cliff to fall headlong into a black hole. If you look closely enough, you might be able to see the Hairy Man's Cave. It's there alright, just beyond the spray and foam of the cascading river, just where the river enters the hole. Look out for it next time you're in Eryri.

A long, long time ago, the people of Nant Gwynant in Eryri were forever being troubled by a thief. He was a cattle-rustler, a poacher, a smuggler—you name it, he was all of those rolled into one. He stole pigs, goats, cattle, sheep, and any animals he left behind he had milked them dry as a bone. He burgled houses, broke into barns and squeezed into granaries and stables. Every night someone or other lost something because of him. He was a stealthy so-and-so and, although he was out every night, he never left a trace of his comings and goings.

One day, one of the Nant Gwynant shepherds was walking down the mountain when suddenly he saw a hairy monster. The monster was lounging in the sun but, at the same time, keeping an eye on a particular house nearby. It was a red-haired monster with long, tousled hair growing over the whole of its body. The shepherd's flesh became like sand-paper, he was so frightened. The shepherd crept slowly along until he had gone past the red monster and was safely inside the house that the monster was watching.

The shepherd quickly told the family what he had seen. The cottage-people were quite certain that the shepherd must have seen the Nant Gwynant thief, biding his time. They all rushed out to catch the crook. The monster was an ugly creature, but the Nant Gwynant army was ready to take him on. However, as soon as the monster saw them, he leapt over the rough land and in no time at all, he had given them the slip. He was nowhere to be seen.

Now that they knew what to look out for, the people of Nant Gwynant were even more determined to catch the thief. Wherever they went, they had one eye open for the red monster and one eye on the road. One day, they saw him again, daydreaming on the Lliwedd, so they set the dogs on him. But, as soon as the red monster heard the dogs, he leapt up and ran for his life. The dogs had no hope of catching him.

Thinking that the red monster must be some sort of spook sent by an enemy to trouble them, it was decided to ask advice of the local wizard. How could they rid the country of the troublemaker?

'There is a way,' said the wizard. 'You must look for a red greyhound. Every hair on its body must be red,' said the wizard, 'or it will be no good to you. Take care of this red greyhound, and the next time you see the red monster, set the red greyhound on him, and he'll be caught—spook or no spook.

The men searched the whole land for a red greyhound. Eventually, they found one in Nannau. It could outrun any hare in the country, and was as red as any dragon's blood, from the tip of its nose to the tip of its tail.

A long time passed without sight or sound of the red monster but they knew well enough that he was still around. Every night the good-for-nothing thief was up to his tricks. But one evening, they spotted him again. He was creeping stealthily along the Lliwedd in the red glow of sunset. It was difficult to see him properly, but it was him right enough. Who else could it be?

They set the red greyhound after him. The hound shot away like greased lightning and he was soon gaining ground but, just as he was

about to nip the red monster's heel, the monster flung himself over a cliff, and bounded away into the red sunset.

Now, the people of Nant Gwynant knew for sure that they had come face to face with a spook. Worse than that, they had failed to catch him—and probably never would. It would make a hard winter, that much was certain.

A baby boy was born in Nant Gwynant. He was a funny little baby, growing by leaps and bounds. It was high time for him to be christened. The family trooped into church, leaving the baby's mother still sick in bed. She lay there quietly after the family had left for the church, thinking about the ceremony. It was a stormy evening and the winds hurtled around the cottage, under the slates on the roof, up the chimney, through the cracks in the window-frames. The door was safely locked, but the mother was still afraid. It was a hard winter and the snow made it difficult to travel. The family was away for a long, long while.

About midnight, the woman heard a commotion outside the back door. Had the wind blown something over? Or was someone, or something, trying to get in? Her fear mounted until she couldn't lie in her bed a minute longer. She was all keyed up and ready for anything. She fetched an axe and stood ready behind the kitchen door. The door opened very slowly, and a red and hairy man's hand reached in through the yawning door. Without fuss or fidgeting, the woman lifted the axe and let it fall onto the man's wrist. The hairy man's severed hand fell to the floor. He rasped horribly and ran away towards the river Erch, croaking and clamouring until he almost cracked his throat.

Before long, the family returned to the cottage having christened the baby boy. No-one had seen the red monster.

'But it isn't a red monster,' said the woman. 'It isn't a spook at all. It's a hairy man, and now it's a hairy man with only one hand.' She showed them the other hand and they were all very impressed.

'We'll hunt him in the morning,' said the eldest son. With that, they all went to bed and slept like logs.

In the morning, the men of Nant Gwynant assembled in the snow to follow the bloodstains left by the hairy man. They expected to see him lying in the snow dead from his wounds. They followed the bloodstains away from the cottage and towards the river Erch. They followed the river until they came to where it tipped itself over the cliff. Still the blood ran on—down the ledge and into a cave behind the waterfall. No-one knew that such a cave existed. This must be the hairy man's cave!

What should they do? Should they set the red greyhound into the cave? No, they had a better idea. If they turned the waterfall into the cave the hairy man would drown, what with all the blood and water. And that is exactly what they did. They changed the course of the river and filled the cave with it. You can still see the cave's mouth, but no-one can go in, or out, of the Hairy Man's Cave to this day.

# The Battle against Saint David

*Way* back in the past, when there were hardly any people living in Wales at all, people used to pass down stories to those who came after them. Many of those early stories were about David, the patron saint of Wales. Once, it is said, a whole army went to fight against him. Who do you think won? I'll tell you.

Saint David and his disciples had been travelling for months on end. They had wandered around the countryside preaching and performing miracles. Out in all weathers, they were getting tired of moving on, staying in a new place for a few days, then moving on again. Saint David decided that the time had come at last for him to settle in one place. He would build a monastery on a piece of land somewhere, and live there in peace with his disciples.

David named a particular day, and promised his friends that wherever they happened to be on the evening of that day, that is where they would stay. Their monastery would soon be up and, in no time at all, they would have a well for drawing water, they would grow wheat in the fields, they would make bread with, and they could spend the rest of their days there, in tranquillity.

On this special day, he and his disciples Aeddan, Teilo and Ismael became very excited. They came to a place called Glyn Rhosyn, just as dusk was falling. This was where their home was to be. Meanwhile, as night drew in, they could do nothing

37

more than eat their bread and drink their water, before falling fast asleep.

A little before dawn on the following day, David woke up. It was a bitterly cold morning, and his limbs were stiff and aching. But he had much to look forward to. His hands wouldn't be numb for much longer. His particular job for the day was to light a fire. This wasn't just any old fire that he had to prepare. It was to be a very special, ceremonial fire. This fire would signify that he, David, was going to settle in the vicinity. Wherever the smoke from his fire travelled, he claimed that land for himself. That was the customary way of claiming ownership. On this land, he would build a simple monastery for himself and his disciples.

He awoke his friends and they hurried to collect sticks for firewood. Their breath trailed white after them, as the pale morning light trickled into the world. Soon, flames were leaping from the mound of wood, and the smoke arose in large clouds, enveloping the whole country and parts of Ireland, from early morning until nightfall. It was very strange.

They weren't the only ones to think so. Prince Boia, an Irishman who owned the land around Glyn Rhosyn, became anxious. He was also in a bad temper. From morning until night, Boia sat on a high rock watching the smoke encircle the land. Boia couldn't eat a scrap of food all day long.

Satrapa, his wife, was a very hard lady. At first, she couldn't find Boia to complain to him about all the smoke that ruined the day for her. Eventually, she found Boia, sitting all alone on his rock.

'Why are you sitting here?' she asked.

'Just watching the smoke,' he said gloomily. 'It's coming from Glyn Rhosyn. There must be someone there. He's claiming the land. Every piece of land and every blade of grass that the smoke encircles will be his.'

'But you can't allow that to happen,' said Satrapa. If she was angry about the smoke before, she was even angrier now. She turned on Boia. 'You must fight this man.' She grabbed his shoulder. 'Stir yourself. Call your men. Kill this person. How dare he light this fire on your land without your permission!'

Boia had no choice but to listen to Satrapa's tirade for the rest of the day. He did as she ordered, calling his soldiers and commanding them to prepare for battle. By the next day, the soldiers' armour gleamed and their horses neighed and reared their heads as the excitement in the camp mounted. They were all eager to kill David and his disciples.

They rode on as far as David's camp. The minute they arrived there, the soldiers' arms went as limp as rags. Their whole bodies sagged with weakness. They shivered and shook and it was as much as they could do to stay in their saddles. A strange disease had gripped them, just as they were ready to attack. They were so weak, they could do nothing to hurt David or his disciples. All the soldiers could do was mock David and shout abuse at his friends. Eventually, the soldiers had to return to their camp, a very sorry sight indeed.

On their return journey, whom should they see coming to meet them but Satrapa. She was in a mad panic.

'Hurry home! Come on, hurry, hurry! A terrible thing has happened!'

'Satrapa! What's the matter?' asked Boia.

'The shepherds tell me that all the animals are dead—every last one of them—the cows, oxen, sheep, stallions and mares—they're all lying dead in the fields, with their eyes wide open.'

Boia was shocked and afraid. His soldiers had been stricken with fever and couldn't lift a finger, and now his entire stock had been struck down in one blow.

'It must have something to do with that man in Glyn Rhosyn', said Boia. 'There must be some connection between the clouds of strange smoke that spread over the country yesterday and these terrible tragedies that have happened to me today.'

Satrapa was inclined to agree with Boia. 'It must all be the fault of that man. What can we do?'

'There's nothing much we can do is there? He must have special powers to be able to perform such miracles. I can only say that I think he must be a saint.

'If he's a saint', said Satrapa, 'it's useless to go against him.'

'Exactly', said Boia. 'I must give him Glyn Rhosyn before anything worse happens to me.'

So Satrapa and Boia, much against their wishes, trudged along to David's camp. They apologized for bringing an army against David and promised that the land around Glyn Rhosyn should be his. David was free to build a monastery there, and to live in peace and quiet with his disciples for the rest of his days. His successors also had permission to settle there for as long as they wished.

Boia and Satrapa were disappointed about their loss, but they were secretly glad to have got off the hook so lightly. But that didn't stop them from mumbling and grumbling, and moaning and groaning all the way home.

When they got within earshot of the palace, they couldn't believe their ears. There was a terrible din coming from the surrounding fields. Their sheep and cattle, oxen and horses, had all come back to life again. They were neighing and mooing, baa-ing and lowing, as only hungry stock can do. And little wonder! They had lost a day's feed!

# Owain's Secret

*Owain* lived in a world of his own. He lived on a farm tucked away in a lonely part of the parish of Llanarthne on Mynydd Mawr.

Owain himself was a loner. Although he was one of a cluster of children, he kept himself to himself. But he was no stay-at-home. Since there were so many children in the family, most of them sons, he soon decided that there were enough pairs of keen hands ready to work the farm without his help. He saw no point at all in shouldering his share of the digging and sowing, weeding and harvesting. No, he preferred to ride his horse, visiting here and there, seeing this and that. Being an easy-going son, he never

worried his fair head over anything. But there was one thing that he was very careful over, and that was his well. He owned a well. It was his very own. It stood in one of his father's fields for all to see. This was his favourite haunt and he often came to the well for a drink, and to water his horse. Then he would sit quietly nearby, musing over his whims and passing the time of day in privacy, apart from his horse, of course, who was his best friend and didn't really count.

This well had a secret. No-one knew this secret except Owain and his father's side of the family, and only the chosen son of every generation on that side. One day the secret was almost out and it was Owain who almost spilt the beans. This is how it happened.

Owain always kept a flagstone over the mouth of the well, a large flat stone to keep the dead flies out of the water. When he and his horse had quenched their thirst, always and without exception, Owain would pull the heavy flagstone across the top of the well. The stones grated against each other and the sparks flew, but Owain persevered. Eventually, the stone was back in its proper place.

But one day, Owain forgot. He forgot to cover the well. It was a sultry day and he and his horse had travelled for miles without seeing a soul to cheer them. Languidly they made for the well, through the buzz of bees and biting horseflies. Dismounting, the well seemed a haven for weary bodies, clear and cold. Both man and beast were satisfied.

And then they rode away! Away went Owain on horseback, forgetting to replace the flagstone. He rode idly in the direction of his home, vaguely thinking of doing some work on that quiet summer evening. It was then that he noticed it. His horse's hooves were wet. They were creating tinkling little splashes as they kicked against trickling water. It hadn't rained for weeks on end and Owain was very surprised indeed. Casually, Owain looked back to see the source of this unexpected water.

It was the well. The water had overflowed the well. It flowed over the flagstone on one side and it would soon drown the whole field. If he didn't act soon, the waters would drown the field, his father's farm, and the whole district, in no time at all. Owain had a mind of quicksilver when he chose to use it so this is what he did.

Owain rode around the water creating a ditch from the track of the horse's hooves. The ditch was soon deep enough to hold all the water that had already spilled out of the well. Owain saw his chance. He sped back to the mouth of the well. Dragging at the flagstone in his wet clothes, his trousers sticking to his legs and water squelching in his boot-legs, Owain mustered his strength. He clung to the stone and heaved. The stone moved slowly, slowly. Still the waters poured out. Soon, the flagstone grated against the mouth of the well, but the bubbling waters almost floated the stone away. Owain dragged at it again, even more forcefully. Slowly the waters subsided, as Owain won the day. The well was calm once again.

Owain wiped his brow in satisfaction, mounted his horse and went home to change his clothes and to pamper his horse. A good day's work had been done. His secret was safe.

47

# Arthur and the Magic Sword

*The* kingdom of Britain was without a king. The dead King Uther had been killed—not in battle, but because his Saxon enemies had poisoned the water in his well. His throne was now empty and there was no-one to reign over the Britons. Worse than that, there was an open quarrel going on as to whom Uther's successor should be. Clashes and bickerings were ruining the realm.

At last, Myrddin called the nobles of the land to a right royal conference in London. Only the aristocracy attended—men of blue blood, each with his own coat of arms, boasting that they were the first families in the land. Their wives looked as if they had been born in

purple, every inch a queen. What a commotion! There was no love lost between them. Each man yearned to be crowned King of Britain before leaving for home.

Imagine their surprise when Myrddin instructed them to pray! They, and the priests of the land, were to pray that God should send a sign to tell them which of the aristocrats should become king. The noblemen were tongue-tied. They had hoped for feasts and dancing and a great deal of showing off—not religion. But they had to buckle down and accept their lot.

They prayed and prayed. By the following morning a large, square rock had appeared outside the conference house. Its centre was shaped like an anvil. They were surprised enough by that. They were more surprised to see a sword in the anvil. There was a message written in gold on the sword which read:

WHOEVER CAN PULL THIS SWORD OUT OF THE ANVIL IS THE RIGHTFUL KING OF BRITAIN.

They all, nobles and priests alike, kneeled down on the spot, and thanked God aloud for answering their prayers. They secretly prayed, too, for strength to pull the sword out of the stone.

After a hearty breakfast, the noblemen lined up to pull the sword. They were of all shapes and sizes—some were sinewy others wiry, some broad-shouldered others cry-babies, some athletic others flabby, many stout, a few seedy, some wishy-washy others sturdy. All attempted the feat, even the worn-out ancients. No-one was going to be left out.

They grunted and groaned as they pulled and tugged, and hauled and wrenched until their biceps and sinews were at snapping point. But no-one managed to free the sword. Myrddin was eventually forced to bring the conference to a close. The noblemen went home bitterly disappointed.

There was nothing for it but go to the country. An open invitation was issued. Anyone who wanted to try pulling the sword from the anvil was welcome to try. And try they did. The whole land came to London to see the stone and no-one left for home without wrestling with the sword. Weather-beaten thugs tried their luck, even the gossamer thin, the rickety-legged, the lame and hobbling, the legless, the eyeless. They all tried, but no-one succeeded.

It was then that Arthur decided that he, too, would test his strength. Arthur was Uth's son, but Arthur's mother was married to another man, Gwrloes, Earl of Cornwall, when Arthur was born. Everyone tried his best not to take any notice of Arthur because his parents weren't married to each other. He was the very last person in the land to try his strength on the sword.

Arthur held the hilt of the sword, and pulled. To his amazement, the blade slid out easily, and Arthur found himself flat on his back. All the spectators rushed up to him as he scrambled to his feet—the new King of Britain.

But no. When the noblemen heard the news, they were very unwilling to crown Arthur king. They insisted that he put the sword back in the anvil so that the aristocracy could make another attempt at pulling the sword out of the stone. And so it was decided. Arthur returned the sword to its place.

Again the nobility grappled with the sword. Again they failed. It was more than a match for the haughty barons. Arthur was called. He had to pull away the sword for the second time, or no-one would believe that he was the rightful King of Britain. If the sword remained locked in the anvil, Britain would be without a king.

Arthur stepped forward. He pondered the palm of his hand for a better grip, and walked towards the square stone. He grasped the hilt of the sword, and pulled. The blade slid smoothly out of the anvil.

'Arthur is King! Arthur is King!

Arthur is King!' shouted the people.
'Long live King Arthur! Long live
King Arthur! Long live King Arthur!'
Even the noblemen joined in the
chanting by the end.

The Archbishop anointed Arthur
king with great pomp and ceremony
and Arthur bore the royal crown of
the realm with great dignity for the
rest of his days.

# The Marriage of Branwen

*Bendigeidfran* was a giant. He was crowned King of the Island of Britain. One afternoon he happened to be in Harlech, at one of his courts. Sitting on Harlech Rock, above the stormy sea, he was accompanied by his brother Manawydan, and two half-brothers on his mother's side, Nisien and Efnisien. Nisien was a peaceful man and would always create peace between the two halves of the family even when they were at loggerheads. Efnisien carried a chip on his shoulder and would generate bad feeling the minute he stuck his nose through the door. There were also a number of crawling courtiers about, as one would expect to see in the presence of a king.

Sitting there on the rock, they saw thirteen ships crossing the sea from Ireland.

'Arm yourselves!' commanded the King. 'These ships are coming at great speed. Go and see what they want.'

His warriors armed themselves and went down to the water's edge. Near at hand, the ships looked magnificent. They were lavishly decorated, with blazing panoply and bearing fine standards of brocaded silk. One of the ships came forward, and they could see on its deck a man holding a burnished shield, its point towards the skies signifying peace.

Bendigeidfran's warriors pushed out to sea to question the visitors. Bendigeidfran could hear everything plainly because their voices carried across the sea and wafted to where he sat on his high throne. Bendigeidfran butted in.

'Greetings!' said Bendigeidfran. 'Who owns these ships?'

'Lord,' they answered, 'they belong to Matholwch, King of Ireland. I am his messenger.'

'What is your message?' asked Bendigeidfran.

'He wants to marry your sister, Branwen,' they answered, 'and so bond together the Island of Britain and Ireland.'

'Then tell him to land,' said Bendigeidfran, 'so that we can discuss the matter.'

And so he did.

There was a great throng in the court that night, feasting and carousing until dawn. The next afternoon a committee was held. They all agreed that Branwen should marry Matholwch. She was one of the Three Chief Ladies of the Island of Britain, and the most beautiful in the whole world. She was to be married in Aberffraw, and to sail from there to Ireland.

The preparations were made and both parties travelled to Aberffraw—Matholwch by sea and Bendigeidfran on land. Soon, the festivities began. Bendigeidfran was so big that he had never been inside a house, so the celebrations were held in marquees. The revelling continued into the small hours but when Matholwch and Branwen decided that it would be better for them to retire, they went to bed.

The following day they housed and stabled all the horses and servants. There were so many of them, they were scattered through every acre of land on Anglesey—to the very sea's limits. With that task behind them, the hosts could enjoy the festivities with renewed vigour.

That day, Efnisien happened to come to where Matholwch's horses were being stabled and, not recognizing them, he asked whose they were.

'These are King Matholwch's horses,' they said.

'Then what are they doing in Aberffraw?' he asked.

'The King himself is here. He married your sister yesterday, and his horses are stabled here for the visit.'

Efnisien's temper flared. He went into a mad frenzy that increased with every syllable. 'How dare they use my sister in such a way! It's a personal insult to me. She's a beautiful woman, and *my sister!* How dare they allow her to marry anyone without my consent?'

At that, he attacked the horses, maiming them savagely, cutting off their lips at their teeth, and their ears at their roots, and their tails at their spine; and where he could, he ripped off their eyelashes, cutting them back to the bone.

The news reached Matholwch.

'Lord,' said his breathless servant, 'you have been grossly insulted. That was their intention all along.'

'I doubt it. It would be very strange of them to allow me to marry such a wonderful girl as Branwen if they meant to insult me. And yet the truth is there for all to see.'

'Lord, it's obvious that that was

Although you must feel mortified, Bendigeidfran is sure to feel it more.

'That may be so, but his pity will do nothing to ease my pride.'

He continued to pack his bags while Bendigeidfran's men hurried back to court.

'We can't let him leave in such a mood,' said Bendigeidfran. 'Go back and offer him a healthy horse for every maimed one, and on top of that a silver stick, as thick as his finger and as long as he is tall, together with a gold plate the size and breadth of his face. Apologize to him, and tell him that it was Efnisien who did these strange things to his horses but that I can't very well kill him since he is my mother's son.'

Matholwch listened to their message and took counsel. They decided to

their intention. All you can do now is retreat.'

He took his servant's advice and commanded his troops to retreat to the ships. But before he could escape, news of his moves had reached Bendigeidfran.

'He has left without my consent. Ask him his reasons.'

The servants caught Matholwch as he was preparing to leave Aberffraw.

'I would never have come near your court in the first place had I known then what I know now,' said Matholwch. 'I have been deeply insulted. No-one on earth has experienced harsher treatment than I have experienced today.' And he related his unhappy tale.

'Lord, it wasn't at Bendigeidfran's command that that happened.

cut their losses and accept the offer. They rode back to Bendigeidfran's tents and pavilions to celebrate the reconciliation by feasting. But that evening, Bendigeidfran felt that Matholwch was somehow not quite his old cheerful self.

'Are you worrying that you have not been given enough money? If so, I'll increase the offer. Added to that, I'll give you the Cauldron of Rebirth; it is very strange and powerful. This magic cauldron can raise up soldiers from the dead. Take it with you into battle. If one of your warriors is killed, throw him into the cauldron. On the second day he'll be as fierce as ever he was, except that he has no voice. The people who come out of the cauldron can't speak a word,'

Matholwch was humoured by this, and felt much happier. The evening passed pleasantly away, until at last, sleep enveloped all.

At daybreak the payment of horses was made, and they rode from district to district until enough horses were found to fit the bill. Then they travelled the area in search of foals so that the insult was redeemed with the price of the young. For that reason, the area was called *Tâl Ebolion*, The Recompense of Foals.

That done, Matholwch and Branwen set off for Ireland from Abermenai, in their thirteen ships.

# Prince March of Llŷn

# *Prince* March

March was a sad man. Although he lived in Llŷn, in a grand palace that overlooked the sea, Prince March was not one bit impressed by anything any more. If anyone praised his soldiers' skills, or admired the treasures in his vaults, he would say 'That's nothing to boast about.' Whatever was done to cheer him up, it was all wasted effort. 'He'll come to a bad end, sure as death,' muttered his men, half afraid that someone would hear them.

Hear them? Someone might indeed. Prince March had horse's ears! He had every reason to be sad with a horse's ear on either side of his head. No-one knew his secret, of course, but he was afraid that some-one might tumble to it one day.

Once a year, he had his hair cut. That was the worst day of the whole year for Prince March. On that day, he had to show his ears to the hair-dresser. Prince March could see the shock on his hairdresser's face very clearly, then the shock became a smile, then a giggle, and to Prince March's acute embarrassment, the hairdresser would split his sides with laughter. Every year like clock-work, Prince March would wait until the hairdresser had finished trim-ming his hair and then he would kill him and bury his body in the marsh outside the castle walls. In time, a fine crop of reeds grew thick and strong right over the collection of hairdressers' bodies. The wind sang its complaint mournfully in the

65

reeds—spring, summer, autumn and winter.

One day, just after having his hair trimmed, Prince March's men persuaded him to prepare a grand feast, hoping that Prince March would cheer up, if only for a minute. Prince March agreed to the feast, and invited all the other lords of Gwynedd to his palace. There were many bards there too, many harpists, and a good number of pipers.

Of all the pipers who came to Prince March's feast, there was one in particular whom Prince March enjoyed listening to. It was Cynan Hen, an old man who lived in the village nearby. Cynan Hen the Piper was second to none. He knew all the local tunes, and a great many new ones too. Prince March had to sit patiently through his feast before he could call on Cynan Hen to play his pipe for him.

Cynan Hen was well prepared for the evening. He had practised hard for days; he had even learned one new melody especially for the Prince. More than that, he had a new pipe. He was going to play his new melody on his new pipe for the first time ever at Prince March's feast. He wondered how his new pipe sounded, and fidgeted on his stool as he sat waiting for his name to be called.

When it was time for Cynan Hen to perform on his pipe, the court was as quiet as death. Cynan Hen put his new pipe to his lips and blew. Nothing happened—Cynan Hen blew harder.

*'Prince March has horse's ears!*
*Prince March has horse's ears!'*

'Cynan Hen's reed pipe sang on and on, repeating its song:

*'Prince March has horse's ears!*
*Prince March has horse's ears!'*

Prince March had never been so angry in all his life. He drew his sword. 'I'll kill you for this, Cynan Hen. I'll kill you for this, this very night.' Cynan Hen pleaded for mercy. 'All I did was try out a new jig on my pipe, and a merry old dance-tune it is too.'

'Bring me that pipe,' Prince March commanded.

'It's a brand new pipe,' said Cynan Hen. 'I made it especially for this evening. I chose the reed carefully. I chose it from the clump that grows under the palace walls. They're the best reeds that I ever set eyes on, and that's the truth.'

Prince March took the pipe. He put it to his lips and blew.

*'Prince March has horse's ears!*
*Prince March has horse's ears!'*

That was the only song the reed pipe knew. 'The song is a true song,' said Prince March sadly. 'That has been my secret until now.' He told the lords of Gwynedd and all the bards, harpists and pipers about his terrible ears, and how he had killed his barbers to make sure they kept his secret and how their bodies were buried under the palace walls. Now they were taking their revenge. Prince March pushed back his hair so that everyone in the hall could see his ears. He expected the revellers to snigger and laugh at him. Instead, they shouted and cheered and were as happy as could be. The hairdressers of the kingdom were no longer a dying race!

# Einion the Shepherd

***Einion*** was the youngest and last of six sons. His father was a shepherd and, from first thing in the morning until last thing at night, Einion was in the fields with his father tending the sheep. In the early spring, Einion was there to see the first lamb being born and, by the time he was ten years old, Einion could help his father deliver a lamb. His hand was slender and strong and, of all the men in the cottage on the mountain, it was Einion who was best at helping lambs to be born.

So it was, in the spring of the year when Einion was seventeen, that his father planned a surprise for him. His father was getting on in age, and

felt the steep climbs to the summit of the mountain getting too much for him. Einion was to shepherd the sheep by himself from that spring onwards.

From as far back as he could remember Einion's constant companion had been Togo, his Cardiganshire sheepdog. Togo was as black as death, except for his white chest and his two white front paws. His shaggy tail wagged constantly. Together, Einion and Togo had walked for miles on end, up and down the uneven slopes, across field after rugged field, down steep quarries, in short, wherever there were sheep in trouble, Togo and Einion found them and brought them back to safety. No wonder they knew the landscape better than they knew the time of day.

Since they knew the land to the inch, imagine their surprise one fine May evening when they saw the mountain path take a left turning when it had always turned to the right. Einion was in a don't-care mood. He immediately followed this mysterious new path. He came to a wooded glen where there were many fairy-rings. Einion turned to Togo hoping that Togo could lead him out of the glen and back to his sheep, but Togo had disappeared.

'What do you want here?' asked a very short man—the shortest man that Einion had ever seen.

'I was just on my way home,' said Einion.

'Then you'd better follow me,' said the man, 'but don't say a word until I give you permission.'

He led Einion deeper into the glen. Soon, they came to an oval-shaped stone. The man tapped it three times with his stick and, to Einion's surprise, the man lifted the stone away. There was a door under the stone and the man led Einion through it into a deep, long tunnel of steps, lighted by peculiar stones in the walls.

'If you follow me,' said the man, 'everything will work out well for you.' Einion took him at his word.

Before long, they came to a magnificent country, with large mansions and palaces as far as the eye could see, each in its own grounds. Einion could see blue rivers sparkling in the distance, dark woods of strong oak trees, large gardens of beautiful flowers, and everywhere colourful birds sang melodious songs, the likes of which

Einion had never heard before in all his seventeen summers.

At last, they came to a palace that was bigger than all the rest. The little man entered through its gates. This was the man's home. Everything in it was made either of gold or of silver.

The man told Einion to sit with him at a golden table. He did so. The table sagged under the weight of all the food. Einion and the man ate as much as their stomachs could hold without bursting. It was the best meal that Einion had ever had in his whole life. When they had finished eating, all the dishes disappeared without anyone moving them. Einion thought he could hear small voices somewhere, but he could see no-one apart from the little man.

'You can talk as much as you like now,' said the man. Einion would have said 'Good' if he could—but he couldn't. His tongue was tied to the bottom of his mouth.

Just then, a lady came into the room. She had three daughters. The daughters looked long and hard at Einion, and started asking him questions. Einion couldn't answer them. At that, one of the three daughters kissed him! He couldn't believe it! But from that moment on, he could chat and answer questions and speak his mind until the early hours of the morning and beyond.

Einion stayed with the man and his family for a year. Although he was quite happy with them, as time passed, he longed to be at home with his own family in his own land. Einion asked the little man to take

73

him home.

'Oh, don't go now,' said the man. The daughter who had kissed Einion wanted him to stay. Before long, however, her father gave Einion permission to leave their magic land. 'But come back very, very soon,' he told Einion. The daughter gave Einion gold and silver presents to take back with him, and jewels and precious stones of all kinds.

When Einion arrived home, his family was overjoyed to see him. They were afraid that Einion had been killed by a wolf, or had fallen down a quarry, when Togo had returned without him. They had a fabulous party to celebrate his homecoming and were sure that he would never be separated from them again. Einion didn't mention his adventures in the land of magic, or his promise to return there soon.

But one moonlit night, Einion kept his word, and returned to the fairy glen. The little man was glad to see him. He took Einion to his wife and three daughters and they were over the moon with delight. Imagine Einion's surprise when the little man told him that Einion was to marry one of the little man's daughters—on that very day! The wedding feast was ready; the fairy bells were ringing. The bride stepped into her wedding dress and Einion married her in no time at all.

Einion and his wife lived together happily. In a while, however, Einion longed to see his own family again. He tried to persuade his wife to come and live with him close to his father's cottage, but she wouldn't hear of it. However, as time passed, she grew used to the idea, and soon she became quite excited at the prospect.

Her father gave his permission for them to leave, although he was sad to see them go. He gave them each a white horse to ride into the land of mortals.

The following morning, as early as the dew, Einion and his wife stood outside the door of Einion's home. The welcome Einion had received on his previous visit was nothing compared to the welcome he and his wife received on that day. When his family heard that Einion and his wife were going to settle in the neighbourhood they were all thrilled and they all stated that there was no-one in all the land as beautiful as the wife of Einion the Shepherd.

# Prince Llywelyn's Hound

# No-one

*No-one* in the world could hunt as skilfully as Prince Llywelyn. One good reason for this was the gift Llywelyn had received from King John of England. It was a very swift and fierce hound. This dog was the best setter that money could buy or hounds could breed. He was named Gelert.

Prince Llywelyn had an only son. This baby son was a miniature of his father and the apple of his eye. Not many people were trusted to look after this baby, but the Prince could rely on Gelert to watch over his son. Gelert was trusted so implicitly, he was allowed to guard the baby in his cradle unsupervised. When the baby slept, Gelert lay quietly at the car-

ved foot of the crib; if he cried, Gelert whined for the nursery maid; if the baby was restless and Gelert caught the scent of wolves, he stalked down his quarry and rent its limbs apart.

One bright morning, Llywelyn decided that he would go hunting with his lords. He decided that he would ride his best hunter and kill a stag for supper. With a blast of his horn, he was away with his dogs and huntsmen. Llywelyn's hounds were instinctive stalkers, and were the talk of the land. Gelert was the leader of the pack, and his surging strength meant that his victim was always run to earth and ensnared. Llywelyn looked forward to a wildly exciting day.

But, by nightfall, Llywelyn was bitterly disappointed. It had been a bad day for Llywelyn. Gelert had failed him in the hunt. Llywelyn had called and called for the leader of the pack but Gelert was far away from the chase. Llywelyn's other hounds were poor substitutes for Gelert. The hillsides rang with the Prince's call, but still Gelert didn't come. The pack was sluggish without Gelert's leadership and the zest had long gone out of the game for Llywelyn and his lords. They returned to the castle after a bad day's sport, longing for warm baths and a lavish feast to revive their spirits for the following day's hunt. Gelert had let them down for the first time in his loyal life's service, and the men needed to be cheered.

The huntsmen returned to the castle. It was wrapped in deathly silence. The maids were in a huddle in the lower kitchens, not daring to continue preparations for a feast. They had heard fiendish noises coming from the young Prince's apartments. Gelert was there guarding the child but his ferocious snarling and bloodthirsty howling had kept the housemaids at bay. When Llywelyn returned it was as if they had been released by a spring, as they all flurried towards Llywelyn with their jumbled tale.

Llywelyn could not make head or tail of their account so, disregarding them, he headed upstairs to see for himself, calling for Gelert as he bounded to the top, taking two stairs at a time. Gelert crouched towards him. Llywelyn couldn't believe his eyes. The dog's hairs were knotted with congealed blood; there were splashes of red on the floor, on the baby's upturned cradle and on the blankets which lay torn and crumpled in a corner. There was no baby there.

Llywelyn was so shocked by the child's disappearance and the disorder of the scene that he lashed out at his wretched dog, who had turned murderer. With black hatred, he slew the hound with his sword, sinking it deeply into Gelert's side.

As the huntsmen stood at the door, they could hear muffled cries of a baby coming from the next room. Their footsteps on the stairs had awakened him and he was crying out for his nurse. Llywelyn was beside himself when he saw what he had done. There, in the next room, lay his child and, at his side, a dead wolf. The wolf was sprawled out on the floorboards, lacerated by

Gelert's claws and fangs, hacked and mauled in the vicious fight for life.

Llywelyn knew now that his hound had done him well that day. Gelert had saved his son from the wolf and had guarded him well. Llywelyn's grief was next to no man's grief.

Gelert was buried in a grave and every honour was given him. His grave can still be seen today, beneath a mound of stones, in the village of Beddgelert in Gwynedd.

# Saint Collen of Llangollen

*The* morning sun shone on Collen as he sat outside his cell on the hillside. His cell was in the shade of a rock, so he often sat meditating in the sunshine some distance away from his door. On this particular day, however, he was dreaming of summer.

Out of the blue, he heard strange voices. Before he could panic or think about what he could give to eat to the owners of those voices, he realised that they were just passers-by on their way to market. But they were not discussing the price of sheep.

'They say that Gwyn ap Nudd must be king over two kingdoms—Annwn, full of demons and evil spirits, and the Fairy Kingdom full of *tylwyth teg*, you know, the mischievous fair folk.'

'Quite so. Quite so. That's why I keep telling all and sundry to keep on his right side. He's a good friend to have. When we draw our last breath, we'll be glad enough of his company then.'

The good hermit could not bear to hear any more. He strode up to them in his brown habit and told them sharply to stop speaking of Gwyn ap Nudd in such glittering terms. 'He's no better than a devil. For shame on you, you disgraceful people.'

The two farmers were rattled. 'Us be quiet? You be quiet yourself unless you want to anger Gwyn ap Nudd. Keep on his right side, that's what I always say.' And, with that, the two men hurried down the slopes to their business.

Collen went to his cell and shut the door on the world and all its ignorant people. Before long, there was a threefold knock on the door and a man's voice called to him: 'Are you at home, Collen?'

Collen was suspicious of all visitors at the best of times, but now that he had just been thinking and speaking of the king of the demons, he was more than ever so. 'Who wants to know?' he called back.

'Gwyn ap Nudd, King of Annwn and King of the Fairies. I'm his messenger. He commands you to meet him on the brow of the hill at mid-day.'

'Is that so?' was Collen's only reply. The messenger went away, to see what noon would bring. Collen went back to his books and did not so much as put a toenail past the threshold that day.

The next morning, although fine and bright, Collen did not sit out in the sun to meditate. He read his books and meditated behind closed doors. But, before long, there came a threefold knock on his gnarled oak door and a voice called to him: 'Are you at home, Collen?'

'I am. Who wants to know?'

'Gwyn ap Nudd, King of Annwn and King of the Fairies. I'm his messenger. He commands you to meet him on the brow of the hill at mid-day.'

'Is that so?' was Collen's only reply, and he returned to his studies. He did not so much as put an eyelash past the threshold that day.

On the morning of the third day,

the same messenger came to Collen's door at precisely the same time, repeating exactly the same message. But he added: 'Collen, you'd better listen to me this time. If you don't come to the brow of the hill of your own free will, Gwyn ap Nudd will drag you up there by the scruff of your neck.'

Collen understood the message and he prepared himself for the walk in the heat of the day. He toiled up the slopes, his mind on what lay before him. In case things became difficult, he had a vial of holy water in his robe pocket. He touched it every now and then for reassurance.

As he staggered up the path, to his amazement he could see a castle on the brow of the hill. There had never been a castle there before. There was also an army of soldiers in gleaming armour. No army had ever been there before. As he neared the castle, he could hear groups in concert, and entertainment of all kinds under the heavens, all in harmony.

The king of this scenario stood a little apart from the merrymaking. He was looking out over his subjects.

Collen was not very impressed by anything he saw. All he wished for was his own cell in the rock's shade. He entered the castle and the trumpets announced his arrival. He was led immediately to the king.

'Greetings!' said Gwyn ap Nudd. 'My two kingdoms wish you well. Look! We've prepared a feast in your honour. Choose any bird, beast or fish to eat and, if there is anything else that you need, just say so and you can have it.'

There was certainly plenty to choose from—meats, exotic vegetables and fruit, nuts, cakes and pastries, honey and nectar, all on gold dishes and in gold goblets. There was a golden throne for Collen to sit on, next to Gwyn ap Nudd himself.

'Stay here for as long as you like. Then, when you return to your hermit's life, you may take whatever you want with you—servants, horses, anything! Come on, now! Eat and drink.'

'I'll never eat the leaves of trees, Gwyn ap Nudd, or drink the dew on the grass, and you know very well what I mean.'

'I do indeed, Collen. But if you stay in my kingdoms, you may wear the liveries of Gwyn ap Nudd. Red and blue are good, bold colours.'

'Bold, yes but not good. Oh! no. I wouldn't wear those colours for riches or kingdoms.'

'I don't understand.'

'Red is for fire and blue is for ice, and you know very well what I mean.'

Collen took the holy water from his robe pocket and sprinkled it over the people, the food and drink, and all that surrounded him. Everything vanished into thin air. Nothing was left but the brow of the hill, quiet and calm as it had always been.

Collen wandered down the slopes again, directing his toenails and eyelashes just wherever he liked.

# Syfaddan, the Submerged City

*During* the days of the Romans, the prince of the city of Syfaddan died a very savage death. His kingdom passed into the hands of the lovely Gwenonwy, his beautiful and strong-willed daughter. She had no qualms about her authority. She would as soon give sentence of death as rock a cradle. Not that she had her own cradle to rock. She was unmarried and had not the least intention either of getting married or of carrying on the lineage for many a happy year.

That is not to say that she had no suitors. She rather enjoyed her suitors. Dozens of eager hopefuls called at the palace, expecting to sweep her off her feet and so win

her love and her riches. She scorned them all and held her head high until one mild autumn evening the son of a prince came to see her. This Gruffudd, although of gentle birth, was very poor, without a stick to call his own.

The haughty Gwenonwy refused him outright. But Gruffudd had a silver tongue and persuaded her to consider his proposal. Although Gwenonwy was powerful, she had her hands tied over the question of marriage in any case. She had promised her father, before his death, that she would never marry a man that was her inferior in rank or in riches. Until that moment her promise to her father had been of no concern at all to her.

Gruffudd's eloquence, however, was hard to resist. He spoke like an angel until Gwenonwy was spellbound. She ached for him. But at heart, she was her father's daughter, and abided by his word. She urged Gruffudd, therefore, to use his wits and win his fortune. In a year and a day, he could return to her and present himself and his wealth to her again.

So off Gruffudd rode to the court of Tewdryg. He became one of Tewdryg's soldiers and, as such, he gained honour and reputation by the metre—but no wealth. He slew mighty warriors. He slid his sword between their ribs and sliced their hearts; he split their skulls until their blood and brains splashed on their breastplates; but he hadn't a penny to call his own, although his name was resplendent throughout the land with honours and much

acclaim.

Presently, the fighting came to an end, and Gruffudd's time was running out. He had a name but no money. No matter, he would return to the city of Syfaddan and to the court of Gwenonwy.

He travelled for some time, until finally Syfaddan was only a day's journey away. He slept that night at a monastery on the mountain, overlooking Syfaddan and Gwenonwy's castle. His sleep was fitful as he tossed and turned on his bed of hay. At midnight, he awoke again. He could hear low whispering from the adjacent room. Sitting up in his bed, he could hear enough to understand that the Prior was expected back from his travels on the following day, carrying gifts of jewels and gold from Hywel, Prince of Cwm-du.

Gruffudd considered himself fortunate to have overheard so prosperous a tale. Enough riches to win the hand of Gwenonwy herself! He lay back on his hard bed, thinking hard and cruel thoughts. He would certainly kill the old Prior for the love of the young Gwenonwy.

And so it was that Gruffudd's hands were stained with the Prior's blood. With his glittering sack of prizes, he entered the hall of Syfaddan Castle and with his name, his wealth and his heroic tale of murder, won the heart of the avaricious Gwenonwy.

But, before he drew his dying breath, the Prior had made known to the monks who his murderer was.

Presently, Father Owain was sent for, from the castle, to officiate at the marriage service of Gruffudd and Gwenonwy. He performed the ceremony and proclaimed them man and wife. But he would not bless the marriage. He proclaimed that the wrath of God would fall on them in the fourth generation because of Gruffudd's murderous heart and because Gwenonwy had condoned his act.

Gwenonwy was enraged. She was the ruler of the city of Syfaddan and therefore would be respected by all and sundry. All! No mere monk would call down the wrath of God upon Queen Gwenonwy.

She threw him into her deepest dungeon and left him there for many callous years. When, in the days of the fourth generation his words did not come true, she planned to sentence him to be burned at the stake. Autumns came and went until, eventually, a great-grandchild was born to Gruffudd and Gwenonwy. When the child was forty days old Queen Gwenonwy arranged a banquet to celebrate the birth of the fourth generation, unharmed. Father Owain was now a very old man but quite persuaded that his words would come true. As he was dragged to the stake he was mocked for his foolishness. The flame was lit and all hope of survival extinguished.

But, as the heat of the bonfire burst into the sky, a grey mist seeped itself far and near and enveloped every man and woman in the city of Syfaddan. Not a centimetre of space escaped the overwhelming greyness.

High on the hill, a monk was watching the city. When the mist cleared, the city of Syfaddan was a lost city, submerged by a huge grey lake that filled the valley. On the grey waters floated a cradle, the last of the line of Gruffudd and Gwenonwy.

The monk went down to the water's edge to save the child, the sole survivor of the city of Syfaddan, and took him to the monastery to nurture. He grew up to be a fine man. Years later, a church in the vicinity was named after him, the Church of St. Gastayn, or Llangasty, and there it stands to this day.

# King Lludd and King Llefelys

*The* moment Lludd was crowned king, he rebuilt the walls of Caer Lludd and built impressive towers around the city. Then he told the inhabitants to build fine houses for themselves, so that no other city had as many luxury homes as they did. Lludd wanted his people to have the best that money could buy.

Lludd ruled over many dominions and cities, but Caer Lludd was his favourite place and it was there that he lived for most of the year. That is why the city was named after him. But when strange people came to live there, then it became known as London.

Lludd was the eldest of four brothers. Lludd's favourite brother was Llefelys because he was the smartest of the pack. When Llefelys heard that the King of France had died leaving an only daughter to inherit his kingdom, he decided that the best thing he could do was marry her. He asked Lludd's help. Llefelys wanted a fleet of ships, and knights in armour, to accompany him to France to propose to the French princess.

The French courtiers and princes met to discuss this new development and eventually agreed that Llefelys would make a suitable King of France. They had wild parties to celebrate and then Llefelys settled down to rule the land wisely to the end of his days.

As time passed, Lludd was getting more and more depressed with his lot. Three scourges had fallen on his country. The first scourge was a foreign nation, Coraniaid, who plagued Britain. They knew everything from A to Z. Never mind how secretive anyone was, the Coraniaid would surely know if anyone breathed or whispered a word about anything. It only had to be whispered in the breeze, and the whole planet knew the tale. As a result, no harm could become them. No-one could oust them from their stronghold, because they knew of the plans before the soldiers knew of them.

The second scourge was this. A terrible scream rent the skies every May Eve. When they heard this scream the men turned ashen with fear, the women miscarried, children lost their senses, and the animals and plants all over the earth became barren.

The third scourge was this. However much food and drink there was at the king's court, even if the cooks had prepared a feast to last a year, they couldn't enjoy any of it, not a cakecrumb, except what was eaten on the first evening.

Lludd had no idea how to rid his kingdom of these scourges. He assembled his chief ministers and asked their advice. They all agreed that Llefelys's help should be sought, and so they sailed hopefully towards France.

The French coastguards were alarmed when they saw such a splendid fleet. Llefelys prepared his own magnificent fleet, ready for action. Llefelys saw one foreign ship pull out in front of all the others. As he watched that ship, Llefelys soon saw his brother's standards waving their way across the sea. Alone, Llefelys sailed towards his brother for a private chat.

When he heard of Lludd's problems, Llefelys was ready for the challenge. They put their heads together and came up with the idea of making a long bronze horn. If they spoke through that, their words couldn't be carried by the wind and the Coraniaid couldn't hear them. So they made a shining horn. But, whatever one brother said through the horn, his words came out the other end as a savage quarrel. Something or someone was sitting inside the horn spitting out filthy language. Llefelys washed out the horn with red wine and the bad spirit inside the shiny bronze horn was lucky to escape alive.

As soon as the brothers could speak without interruption, they set to solving the problems. Llefelys thought long and hard about the Coraniaid, then gave Lludd special insects. Lludd was to keep some of the insects alive in case the scourge returned the second time; the others he was to crush in water, and sprinkle on the Coraniaid.

'How can I do that?' whined Lludd. 'It's impossible.'

'Of course it isn't,' replied Llefelys. 'Hold a banquet! Pretend you want to make peace with the Coraniaid! Then sprinkle the magic water over everyone. It will poison the Coraniaid but your own people will be unharmed. Easy!'

'The second scourge on your kingdom,' Llefelys explained, 'is a dragon from a foreign kingdom. It's fighting your own dragon until it screams. When you return home, wear stout shoes and take a long walk; measure the length and breadth of your lands to find the centre point. Start digging there. Put a vat of the best mead in the hole and cover it with a silk veil. Keep watch on this spot. Soon, you'll see the dragons fighting in the form of beasts. Then they'll fight in the sky disguised as dragons. When they're tired of fighting, they'll fall on the veil in the form of two piglets, sink to the bottom of the vat taking the veil with them, drink every drop of mead, and sleep like two logs. Wrap them up in the veil immediately, and bury them in a stone coffin deep in the earth at the safest spot in your kingdom. You'll never have trouble with a scourge of that kind ever again while those two are under-ground.'

Llefelys was warming to his subject. 'The third scourge,' he said, 'is a magician who steals your food and drink. He casts a deep sleep over everyone. You personally must keep watch over your feasts. In case he casts his sleeping-spell over you, keep a bath of ice-cold water close by and jump into it when you feel drowsy.'

The brothers shook hands. Lludd set sail for home. He crushed half the wondrous insects in the water and sprinkled it over everyone in the kingdom. At once, the Coraniaid withered and died.

Encouraged by this success, he measured the length and breadth of his kingdom and fixed the centre point at Oxford. There he dug a pit and put a vat of the best Llannerch-y-medd mead in it and covered the vat with a silk veil. That night he kept personal watch over the pit. True enough, the dragons fought and fought. When they were quite exhausted, they fell on the veil, dragging it with them to the depths of the pit. They drank the mead and slept; Lludd wrapped them in the veil and buried them in the safest place he knew—in the solidity of Dinas Emrys in the mountains of Eryri.

Following this, King Lludd arranged a marvellous banquet, with drummers for entertainment. He set a bath of icy water near his throne and watched the feasting. At about the third watch of the night, the drums rolled to a halt. Instead of the drumming, he could hear strange melodies forcing him to sleep. Armed as he was, he sat in the cold bath every now and then to prevent himself from dozing off.

In the dead of night, a giant in heavy armour appeared carrying a hamper and he filled it with the food and drink. He crammed in the pies and pasties for all he was worth. Lludd was astounded at his cheek. He attacked the giant fiercely and they fought until the sparks bounced from their armour. Fate favoured Lludd and he flung his enemy on the floor until he could only cry for mercy. From that moment on, the giant was loyal to King Lludd until his dying day.

That is how King Lludd rid his kingdom of the three scourges.

# The Lady of Llyn-y-Fan Fach

*Many* moons ago, when riches were riches and poverty was just poverty, there lived a good man and his good wife on a farm called Blaensawdde at the foot of the Black Mountain. In time, the good man died, leaving his widow and only son to tend the farm. He was a handsome son, with dark brown eyes and curly black hair.

One day as the son drove his mother's cattle to graze the slopes of the Black Mountain, he took them further than he had anticipated. In no time at all, he was almost at the edge of Llyn-y-Fan Fach, a very deep lake. Of course, he had been there many times before, and so he looked for his favourite stone and sat down to watch the cattle graze.

It was the hottest afternoon of that summer and his eyelids closed in sleep. Soon, an unusual lowing awoke him and indeed he was as surprised as the cows to see a beautiful lady standing in the lake. He went down to the water's edge to splash his face with cold water but still he saw the same beautiful woman standing in the lake, watching him. She smiled and began singing to herself, combing her curls with a golden comb.

Seeing her smile, he offered her some of his food—a piece of crusty bread. She glided towards him and held out her hand but, when she saw the burnt crust, she put her hand in her pocket. She laughed and said:

*Cras dy fara!*
*Nid hawdd fy nala.*

105

Not for *her* burnt bread, thank you. With two shakes of her curls, she disappeared into the lake.

It was an extremely confused young man who walked down the slopes of the Black Mountain that evening, and he drove a very bemused herd of cattle before him.

That night, seeing that he ate no supper, his mother wondered what was the matter.

'You sit here with eyes as big as moons, making two bites of a cherry. What's bitten you?'

He told her of the strange lady who had appeared on Llyn-y-Fan Fach.

'Who can she be?' asked the puzzled son.

'She can only be one of *them*,' said his mother knowingly. 'If you want to make a catch of her, you'd better take some bread with you again tomorrow, soft bread, and see if that will tempt her.'

Bright and early with the dew, he gathered the cattle and drove them up the Black Mountain. Soon he was seated on his favourite stone, waiting for the lady of the lake to appear. He waited and waited. It became so hot and sultry on the summer mountain, his eyelids closed in sleep. Then he was awakened by an unusual lowing sound. Before he could open his eyes, he knew that *she* was standing on the lake.

Rushing up to her, he almost forced his bread into her hand.

*Llaith dy fara!*
*Ti ni fynna'.*

Not for *her* unbaked bread, thank you. With two quick blinks of her eyelashes, she was back in the lake.

The scatterbrained young man retraced his steps down the Black Mountain with his herd of scatter-brained cattle. The good woman of Blaensawdde stood watching, but could see only the same expression on her son's face as she had seen on the previous day.

'This evening I'll bake my usual batch of bread', she determined. 'None of this soft bread nonsense and crusty loaves.'

She baked a moderate loaf and gave it to her son.

The next morning, he drove the cattle to graze the same spot, sat on the same stone, and waited. The sun shone on his dark eyes, and shone and shone until they slowly closed in sleep. When he heard the cattle low-ing strangely, he shifted from his stone and was at the water's edge in a trice. The lady was there.

'Take this bread,' he pleaded. 'It isn't too hard or too soft. Take it.'

She smiled, and glided towards him. She nodded and took it.

'I'll marry you. But mind, if you hit me three times without cause, I'll go back to my father for ever and ever.' With that, she disappeared into the ripples of the lake.

In a few minutes, the lord of the lake appeared with his twin daughters. He was a grand and noble man, dressed superbly in a white tunic and purple mantle, with brooches bearing his insignia on his shoulders. The twin daughters were as similar as a double reflection. The star-struck youth could not for the life of him choose between them.

'Which of my two daughters have

you fallen in love with?' asked the lord of the lake. One of the daughters kicked the hem of her dress with her foot, showing her sandal, while the other daughter was barefoot. He remembered seeing the golden straps of her sandals and took this to be a sign.

'I love this daughter best,' he said firmly.

'That is a wise choice,' said the lord of the lake. 'As a wedding present, I'll give you strong herds of my best cattle.'

With that, the youth gathered his mother's star-struck herd and drove them down the Black Mountain, followed by his wife, and herds of strong cattle, which came dripping out of the lake and leaving pools of water on the slopes of the mountain, as they shook their coats dry on

their unaccustomed journey downhill in the sunshine.

The good woman of Blaensawdde watched the procession from her threshold and was happy.

For many, many years, all was peace and prosperity. Their new home was made at Esgair Llaethdy and three sons were born to them there. It seemed as if nothing could spoil their good fortune, not even the threat of the three blows.

One spring, the couple were invited to a christening party. Spring came late that year and the wife was behind with the cleaning, behind with the scrubbing and behind with the clearing. She was behind with the garden and, all in all, everything piled in on her and she was quite vexed about it. Certainly, she did not feel like jaunting away to a christening party on a perfectly glorious day in spring. But, change her work-clothes she did and soon she was standing on the threshold, pretty as a child, awaiting the horses that would take them to the christening ceremony.

'My, you're a grand sight,' said her husband, bringing up the horses. 'You're the prettiest wife anyone ever saw in this whole wide world,' he said.

'I'd much rather be in my old glad rags washing the blankets,' she said, 'with warm white suds up to my elbows.'

'Oh, come on,' said her husband. 'I'm looking forward to be finger-deep in cold white cream—just think of those cakes and crumpets,' and with that he struck her gently with his gloves on her shoulder.

'Christening-time is a beginning, and you too have proved today the beginning of your grief. You have hit me without cause for the first time.'

The husband was very sad that this had happened. He vowed to be even more careful in future. If such a harmless blow had such an effect on her, then he would have to watch his ways.

For months he was watchful and careful, handling her with deep respect and forever being consciously gentle in his ways. Time wore on and even the most determined folk forget with time. Things became normal once more at Esgair Llaethdy and life became sweet.

It was springtime again, and that gave way to a heady summer. Being a popular couple, they had been invited to a summer wedding, and since all the chores were done, they looked forward to it. It dawned just as it should. There was not a cloud in the whole wide sky. Soon they were ready; she was standing eagerly on the threshold waiting for the carriage to take them to the wedding. She looked as happy as a child.

But not for long. Like a child, her mood suddenly changed. When everyone else was at their most cheerful, she was most subdued until, at the height of the party celebrations, she burst into tears. Embarrassed, her husband tried to console her. He tapped her arm with his gloves hoping that she would calm down. 'Please don't cry today of all days,' he urged her. 'This is a happy day for all of us. Please don't cry.'

'Today is a sad day for them and for us. It's the beginning of *their* troubles and the confirmation of *ours*. That's the second time that you've struck me without need.'

Again the husband vowed to be even more careful than he had ever been before. He tended her, looked after her, and would have wrapped her in cotton if he could. The third blow meant death to their marriage. But time wore on. He became a touch more lax in his ways, and life was sweet once again.

And so the years passed. One year, at springtime, a neighbour died and they attended the funeral. She looked stunning in her black mourning clothes, her fair curls peeping through and under her black veil. The black carriage picked them up and soon they were surrounded by sorrow.

The widow and her daughters were as miserable as could be. Imagine everyone's surprise when the wife of Esgair Llaethdy had the gall to start laughing and giggling as heartily as she could. Shock rippled through the gathering, and the husband was mortified. He looked at her, frowning fiercely, but she could not stop guffawing. He tapped her arm but she could not or would not calm down for the life of him.

'Please don't laugh,' he pleaded with her. 'This is their saddest day ever. Please don't laugh.'

'This spring is indeed the saddest time for them and for us. I was laughing for the dead man—all his troubles are now over. And so is our marriage. That was the third time that you struck me without cause.

'I'm going back to my father.' She left the house and kissed him goodbye. Quickly she returned to Esgair Llaethdy and kissing goodbye to her three strong sons, she called together her cattle and all her stock and set off for Llyn-y-Fan. Even the little black calf that had just been slaughtered and was hanging from a hook in the cool-house ran to her side, and they all returned in a long procession behind the lady of the lake. She called to them all:

'Brindled cow, white speckled,
Spotted cow, bold freckled,
The four-field sward mottled,
The old white-faced,
And the grey Geingen,
With the white Bull,
From the court of the King;
And the little black calf

Tho' suspended on the hook,
Come thou also, quite well home!'

. . . and they all followed her voice.
The four grey oxen ploughing the
field left their furrow and, dragging
their plough behind them, back into
the ripling lake they went, and were
never seen or heard again.

Soon after, the husband of Esgair
Llaethdy died of a broken heart. The
sons, however, did not despair. They
often walked the edge of the lake,
hoping to see their mother. One
night, when the moon was at its
brightest , she appeared to them
near Dôl Hywel at the mountain
gate—Llidiart y Meddygon, as it is
now called. She was as beautiful as
ever in the moon's radiance. She
urged her sons to study the art and
science of curing the sick and of

healing bones.

They set to learning, meeting their
mother regularly near the banks of
the lake. Once, she even accompanied them home as far as Pant y
Meddygon, the Physician's Dingle.
There she taught them about various
herbs and flowers and the healing
powers of nature. And that is how
these three brothers became the best
doctors in the land, and they became
famous as the The Physicians of
Myddfai.